To my two wonderful sons, Arran and Lewis who provided the inspiration, support and encouragement for creating this story.

Thanks to Heather and Margaret for their invaluable advice and feedback.

A special thank you to Mandy for all her patience and understanding during the whole illustrative process.

First published 2021 by Distant Light Entertainment
www.distantlight.uk

DISTANT LIGHT ENTERTAINMENT

Design and Branding by Arran Sinclair
www.arransinclair.co.uk

ISBN 978 1 9168838 0 2

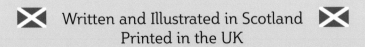

Written and Illustrated in Scotland
Printed in the UK

DISTANT LIGHT ENTERTAINMENT

THE ADVENTURES OF Johnny Groat

THE DISCOVERY

WRITTEN BY COLIN SINCLAIR

ILLUSTRATED BY MANDY SINCLAIR

"WAKE UP!!!" cried Arran. The excitement of his voice filled the motorhome. His younger brother, Lewis, jumped with a start, bumping his forehead on the top bunk knocking him off the side of the bed and onto the floor.

"Owww!" he squealed.

"Did you hear the thunder and lightning last night?" Arran asked excitedly.

"Yeah, it was scary," replied Lewis. "I felt the whole place wobble like a jelly backwards and forwards in the wind."

They both rushed to the large window and pulled back the curtains.

"OH WOW!" they cried.

It was a beautiful Spring morning - the dark clouds from the day before had disappeared and the sun shone over the sleeping Scottish village of John O'Groats.

The caravan site now overlooked a scene of devastation. Keen to get out and explore the boys grabbed a quick breakfast of burnt toast and orange juice and ran outside.

"Don't get up to any mischief," shouted Mum,
"and remember to be back by teatime."

The boys sauntered down the small hill to the beach and saw what could only be described as an absolute mess.

"Over here," shouted Lewis, "Look!"

Washed up along the beach were bits of old rope, tangled fishing nets, plastic buckets, tin cans, two soft footballs, a few ripped shoes, a rusty bicycle, a tractor tyre and wood, lots and lots of wood.

"There's enough wood here to fix Dad's shed," Arran joked.

Frothy foam made by the stirring up of the sea water was spread out along the length of the beach.

Lewis kicked the foam into the air and watched it fly off a short distance. It landed on a huge pile of **sticky, stinky, slimy** seaweed. Arran noticed that sticking out from under the seaweed was a pair of scabby old boots.

Giggling at them he shouted, "Do you want some boots?" As he bent down to pick them up, the boots suddenly moved.

"Ahhhhhh!"

Arran jumped back in horror. Without warning a terrible groaning noise could be heard coming from the **sticky, stinky, slimy** pile of seaweed.

"Wh... wh... what's that noise?" trembled Arran.

"Aaaargh... OOwwww!" went the sound again.

"It's coming from the seaweed," mumbled Lewis.

They stood and watched in shock and amazement as, ever so slowly, bit by bit, the pile of **sticky, stinky, slimy** seaweed began to change shape and move on its own.

Suddenly, out from the top of the tangled mess a long pole began to poke out and creep towards Arran and Lewis who tried their best to remain calm. They wanted to run away but it was as if their feet were stuck in the sand. They couldn't move.

The pole that stuck out was about the same length as their Mum's broom handle but attached to one end was a shiny arrow shaped metal object that glistened in the morning sun.

"Take my spear," said a rather gruff, croaky voice.

Nervously, Lewis leant over and gently got hold of the wooden pole from the grasp of a large hairy wrinkly hand - the kind of wrinkles you would see on your own hands if you spent a long time in the bath.

"Now help me up!" demanded the voice.

The boys looked at each other both feeling very afraid.

"Let's get this seaweed off," said Arran.

They placed their trembling hands carefully into the cold, wet, **sticky, stinky, slimy** seaweed.

"Yuuuckkk!!" they both moaned.

The two brothers slowly lifted big handfuls of disgustingly smelly seaweed from the pile and tossed it over to one side.

It wasn't long before the outline of a large round football shaped object could be seen. With a deep breath Lewis carefully removed the last piece of the **sticky, stinky, slimy** seaweed which lay on top. He wasn't prepared for what they saw next...

A wide and somewhat rounded nose poked out from a rugged, wrinkled and weathered red bearded face.

"It's a man!" stammered Lewis.

The boys watched as droplets of sea water ran down his forehead and into his wild untamed red hair that lay tangled amongst the shells and sand. His bushy red eyebrows sat above his tightly closed eyes like two big hairy caterpillars. His thick red lips began to move.

"Thank you," said the stranger politely.

He opened his large brown eyes and smiled.

"What land is this?" he asked in a muffled voice.

"This is Scotland," answered Arran, "The top of Scotland, John O'Groats to be precise. It's where the road ends. In fact, you can't get much further north on the mainland."

"Scotland you say?" asked the stranger looking puzzled.

Lewis grabbed the stranger's arms and helped him sit upright leaning his back on some of the broken wood nearby. His tattered brown leather outfit, all frayed, torn and wet, stuck to his chubby belly and strong muscular legs. His clothes reminded Lewis of an old film he had once seen that featured Gladiators fighting in a big arena.

"Where are you from and how did you end up here?" asked Arran.

The man looked blankly out at the now calm sea.

"I don't know what happened," he said sadly. "I can't remember...... one minute I was in my boat and the next I woke up here...... all I know is that I don't belong here."

He paused and thought for a second.

"Have you found my little rowing boat?"

The brothers looked at each other and then at their new companion.

"Look around you," said Lewis pointing to the planks of wood and wreckage scattered across the beach. "Is this your boat?"

Their friend, taking a closer look at the wood in front and behind him, sighed and with a tear running down the side of his rosey red cheek he said gloomily,

"Yes, that's my boat."

They all paused for a moment in silence. The reality of the situation hit them like the waves smashing against the rocks. Saddened by their findings, Lewis looked blankly at Arran.

"What now?" he quizzed. "We can't leave him here on his own."

Turning to the stranded stranger, Arran reached out one of his wet sandy hands and rested it on the man's shoulder. Then leaning forward he whispered sympathetically into his rather dirty, hairy ear where grains of sand glittered within.

"Don't worry," he said. "Everything is going to be ok," nodding his head reassuringly, "We'll look after you."

He could feel the stranger's whole body tremble. He could also smell a distinct aroma of rotten fish and **sticky, stinky, slimy** seaweed. The nearer his nose got to his new acquaintance the worse it got.

"Ewwww! You need a bath," exclaimed Arran in horror.

"THE CAVE!" shouted Lewis suddenly in sheer excitement. "We can take him to the cave. It's got fresh water, it's sheltered, it's partly dry, it's a bit cold maybe but it'll do for a little while at least."

Arran remembered that previously while out exploring one day they'd stumbled upon a massive cave carved in the cliff face just up the coast from their motorhome and around the corner out of sight from public eyes.

"Good idea," responded Arran, "but how will we get him there? He's too weak to walk."

"What about that!" suggested Lewis, his arm outstretched pointing to something on the shoreline. He started running towards an old rusty, bashed wheelbarrow that lay upturned on the sand like a grey seal basking in the sun.

Arran prepared the man for the short journey to the cave by freeing him of the **sticky, stinky, slimy** seaweed and rope that remained entangled all around him.

"What's your name?" asked Arran.

The man went deep in thought for a moment; his memory still partly lost by being tossed around in his boat during the storm. Scrunching up his sweaty face and running his hand through his matted red hair he let out some strange sounds,

"J… Ju… Ja… Jun," he stuttered trying to remember.

"JOHN! Is it John?" shouted Lewis as he approached, dragging the rickety old barrow behind him in the soft sand.

The man's face lit up and shone like the brightest star in the sky. His eyes widened like huge dinner plates.

"It's Johhnnn… Jooohna… Johnnnyeahh," he spluttered.

Lewis stopped for a moment.

"Oh! I know, I know!" he exclaimed excitedly, "Is it Johnny?"

An enormous smile filled the man's face. Lewis knew then that he'd guessed correctly.

"Johnny it is then," he said.

With all their strength the brothers lifted Johnny like a sack of potatoes into the wheelbarrow and headed off creaking and rattling towards the cave. A wide dark opening in the cliff like the mouth of a whale ready to swallow them up appeared bigger and bigger the closer they got but once inside it looked truly magical.

High above their heads water cascaded down crashing into the enormous pool below making the sound of a steam engine chugging and hissing along a rail track. Little narrow passages led off into the dark unknown. Stalactites hung down from the roof like Christmas decorations while stalagmites rose from the ground like candles all joining on to each other forming the shapes of what looked like hard rocky furniture.

"This is perfect," said Lewis.

The boys felt very pleased with themselves in getting Johnny to safety. They helped him out of the barrow and propped him up against the dusty wall of the cave.

"Now you stay here and rest," ordered Arran. "Lewis and I are going to get you some bedding for the night, we won't be long."

Johnny looked up at them and nodded his head wearily.

"Be careful of the deadly piranhas in the water," joked Lewis.

The boys ran from the cave, howling with a deafening laughter that echoed throughout the vast empty cavern.

After a refreshing swim in the pool, Johnny began hunting down fish with his sharp spear like a prehistoric caveman. He looked at his catch curiously,

"Piranha?" he chuckled to himself, "piranha indeed," he said roaring with laughter causing him to lose his balance and nearly fall back into his makeshift swimming pool.

Johnny settled himself down in front of his carefully constructed campfire that he had built using bits of wood he'd found around the entrance to the cave. He had clearly made fires in the past because by simply rubbing two long sticks together he was able to make smoke which developed into flames that lit the fire. Johnny sat and waited patiently for his fish to cook for dinner. The fire crackled like a bowl of puffed rice as the small branches popped and snapped from the heat within.

The boys soon returned carrying a comfy sleeping bag, a tartan blanket, a bottle of fresh spring water and a bag of popcorn.

"Look! He's sleeping," whispered Arran softly, "We can't stay, Mum and Dad want us back for tea."

He prodded Johnny gently with a piece of nearby driftwood.

"We've brought you some stuff," he said, still whispering so as not to alarm Johnny. "See you in the morning, goodnight Johnny."

"SLEEP TIGHT JOHNNY!" shouted Lewis, unaware that his loud cry might disturb his sleepy friend.

"Shhhhhh!" replied Johnny bringing his finger up to his lips. "Night night and thank you boys."

The following morning was as beautiful as the day before. Arran and Lewis were up early and eager to see their newfound friend. To their horror, however, they found locals and visitors huddled together in small groups around the village. They were exchanging stories they had heard about a mysterious figure seen wandering around on the beach.

"It's a mermaid!" insisted one person.

"No! it's a sea monster!" exclaimed another, "I've seen the tracks in the sand, it's got four legs and a tail."

Arran and Lewis both realised that they must warn Johnny and started to head off to the cave but they suddenly stopped, their feet sliding on the slippy gravel path as they did. The sound of scraping sandpaper filled the air as the dust from the ground rose from behind the heels of their shoes like smoke. They both stood still, their mouths wide open and their eyes almost popping out of their heads because coming over the hill and getting closer was a strange dark figure silhouetted against the light of the morning sun and it was heading straight for the middle of the village.

"Ohhh Nooooo!" stuttered Lewis rather nervously, **"Johnny!"**

With steady strides Johnny walked confidently along the winding path, his head held high. The woollen tartan blanket the boys had taken to him the night before rested securely on his broad shoulders and hung down his back like a magnificent cloak. He looked quite regal as if he was King for the day ready to greet his public. He appeared happy and grateful to be alive. However, his confidence was suddenly replaced with unease and his walk reduced to a slow shuffle on seeing the number of people that were standing and staring back at him as he approached the crowd. The locals were used to visitors passing through who looked a bit different. Johnny didn't exactly blend in but then people looked as strange to Johnny as Johnny did to them.

Within a short time, people became curious about this strange visitor and began asking him questions and accepting him for who he was. Arran and Lewis were delighted with Johnny's warm welcome.

After a day or two, Johnny was asked to tell his tales to the tourists and visitors who flocked to John O'Groats. He soon became quite a celebrity in the village bringing joy and laughter to all who encountered him.

One day when leaving one of his storytelling sessions he decided to go for a little walk to the famous signpost but his walk was quickly interrupted when he felt the back of his tunic being tugged fiercely, Tug... Tug... Tug... Surprised and shocked he turned around. There before him stood a little girl, her hair tied in pigtails. She looked up at him with a shy smile and said timidly,

"Please sir, what's your name?"

With a loud chuckle, loud enough to fill a school hall he looked up at the signpost before kneeling down to the girl and said proudly in a deep gruff voice,

"My name is Johnny, Johnny Groat."

Visit Johnny Groat Online
to discover more!

www.johnnygroat.co.uk

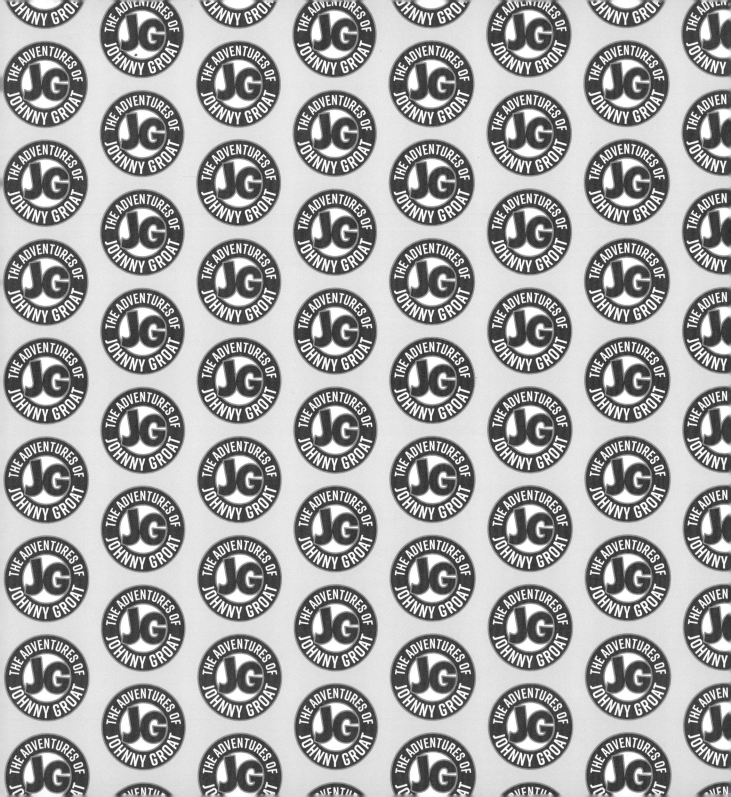